Petah
and the
Big Blue Sea
by J. I. Spencer

Petah
and the
Big Blue Sea
by J. L. Spencer

There was a place near the shore
called the Kingdom of Minn,
where little fish did their chores
'til it was time to go in.

If the fish did their best,
when they grew big, they could be,
picked to live the Great Life
in the Big Blue Sea.

There were three groups of fish,
for whom the bell tolled.
The best of the bunch
was the Seaweed Patrol.

The Seaweed Patrol
had a fun job to do.
They just swam all day
and gathered seaweed for food.

The second group
had a job that wasn't fun.
They were called the Roof Scrubbers.
It took all day to scrub one!

The third group was Stone Sentry.
They were the strongest of all.
They protected the kingdom
by rolling stones to the wall.

One little fish named Petah
was blue with a green tail.

He was strong, he was fast,
he was smart as well.

Petah's job was Stone Sentry,
alongside Reynard.
Reynard was strong
and always worked hard.

Petah would roll a few stones
with barely a care.
Then he'd go find his friends
and leave Reynard there.

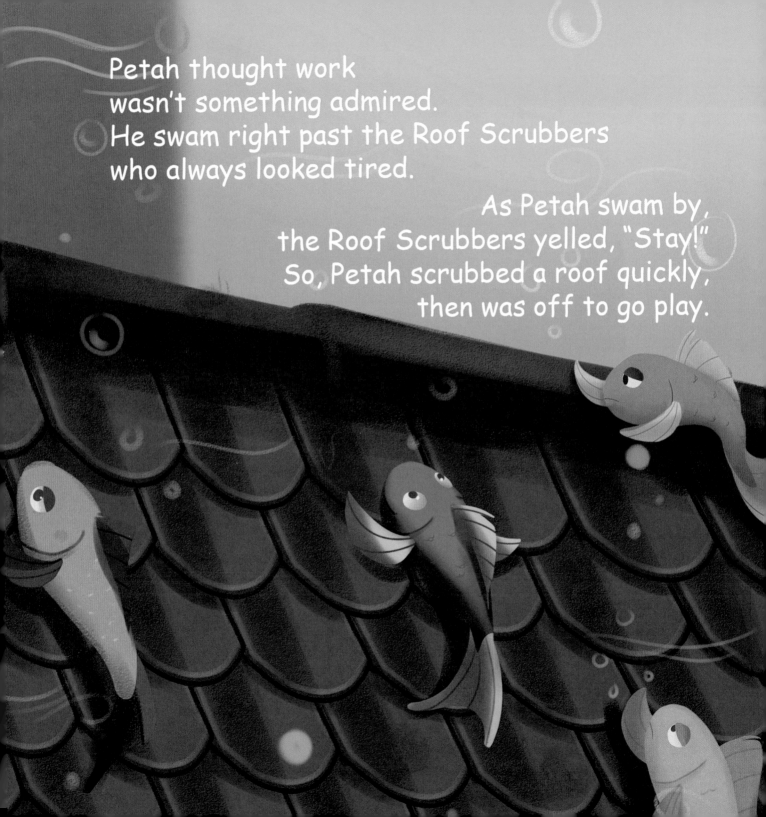

Petah thought work
wasn't something admired.
He swam right past the Roof Scrubbers
who always looked tired.

As Petah swam by,
the Roof Scrubbers yelled, "Stay!"
So, Petah scrubbed a roof quickly,
then was off to go play.

In a seaweed patch,
Petah met with his friends,
Rocky and Sheena,
the Seaweed Patrol twins.

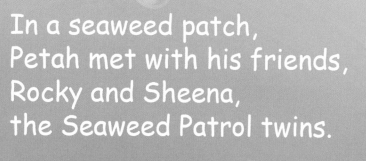

While the twins worked hard,
Petah swam all about.
He laughed, and he played,
but barely helped out.

Six months passed by.
The Kingdom of Minn was excited.
It was time for the Best Fest.
This was when Queen Fish decided.

Queen Fish would pick
from all little fish.
The ones who were picked
got their Big Blue Sea wish.

Petah felt he would win.
He could scrub roofs and
roll stones.

He even helped with seaweed
'til it was time to go home.

That night, Petah was excited.
He could do it all, it seemed.
He fell asleep with a smile.
"I'll be a Big Fish," he dreamed.

"I'm good enough at everything.
Queen Fish will choose me.
I'll get my wish to live life in the Big Blue Sea."

It was early next morning, and all was serene, 'til the Seahorses blew trumpets announcing the Queen.

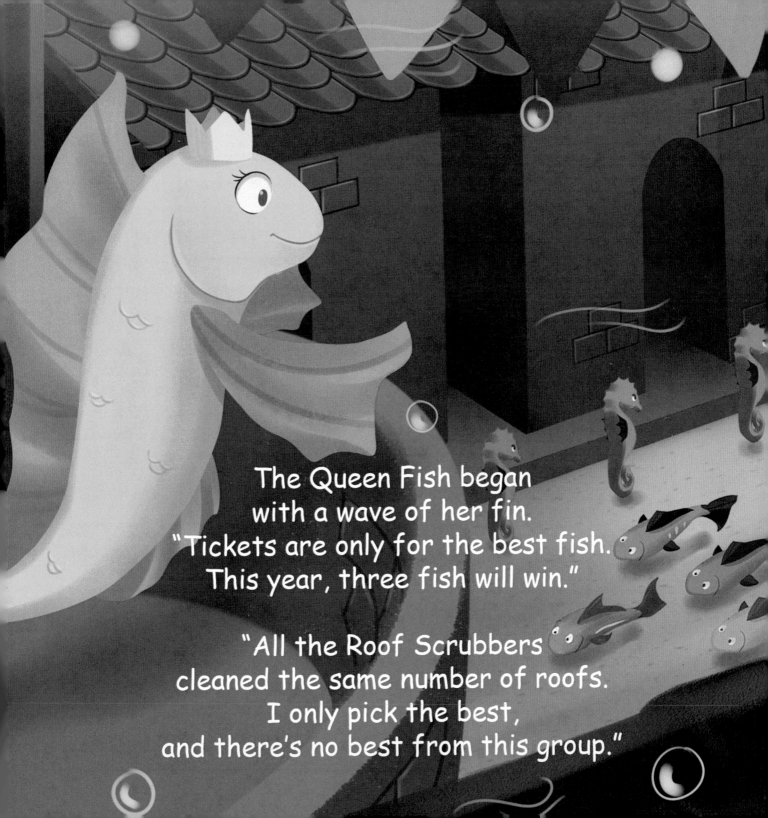

The Queen Fish began
with a wave of her fin.
"Tickets are only for the best fish.
This year, three fish will win."

"All the Roof Scrubbers
cleaned the same number of roofs.
I only pick the best,
and there's no best from this group."

"Two fish helped each other,
and both reached their goal.
The winners are Rocky and Sheena
of the Seaweed Patrol."

As the crowd cheered,
Petah thought to himself,
"I will win the last ticket.
I can think of no one else."

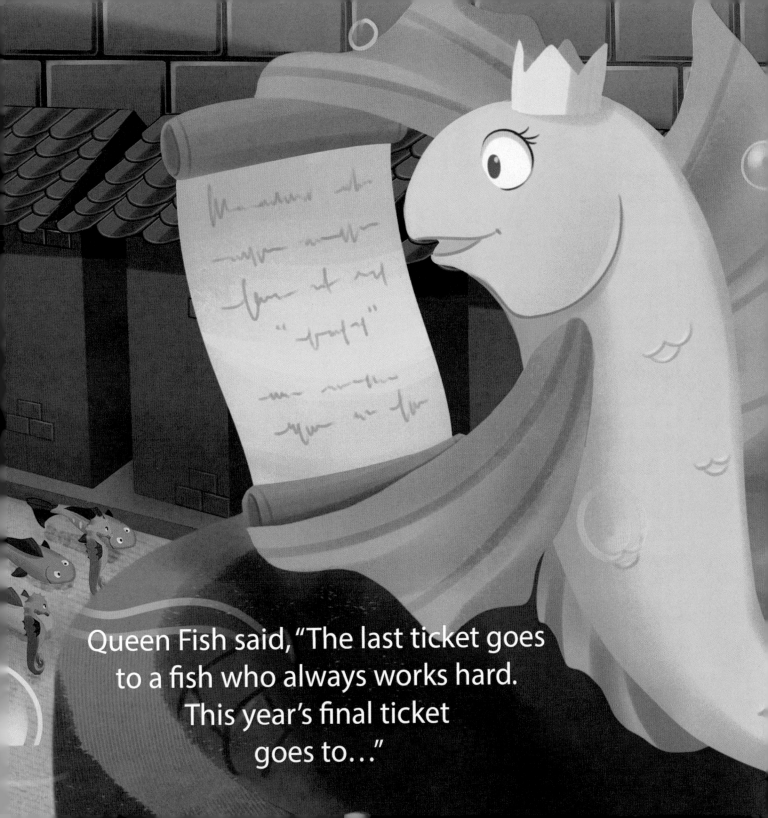

Queen Fish said, "The last ticket goes to a fish who always works hard. This year's final ticket goes to…"

"...Reynard!"

Everyone cheered.
Reynard did his best every day.
Reynard earned his ticket,
and he earned it his way.

Petah was stunned.
"But I am Petah," he thought.
"I'm good enough at everything.
That's good enough, is it not?"

The announcements were done.
There was a celebration to be had.
Petah smiled on the outside,
but on the inside, he was sad.

While everyone partied,
Petah snuck out the door.
Petah didn't feel like partying
at all anymore.

The next day, the four friends said their goodbyes.
Rocky, Reynard, and Sheena had won the big prize.

As they turned to swim away, Petah asked Sheena, "Gee, will I ever win a ticket to the Big Blue Sea?"

"You're a talented fish," his friend Sheena replied. "But you must learn to do your best, Petah. I truly hope you decide."

Sheena was right.
He could be the best at something, he could.

But, what did he like to do?
Which group needed a fish to do good?

"The Roof Scrubbers!" he exclaimed.
Petah scrubbed faster than the rest.
Though it was not a fun job,
Petah could be the very best.

Petah decided
to start right away.
He wanted to do his best.
There was no time to play.

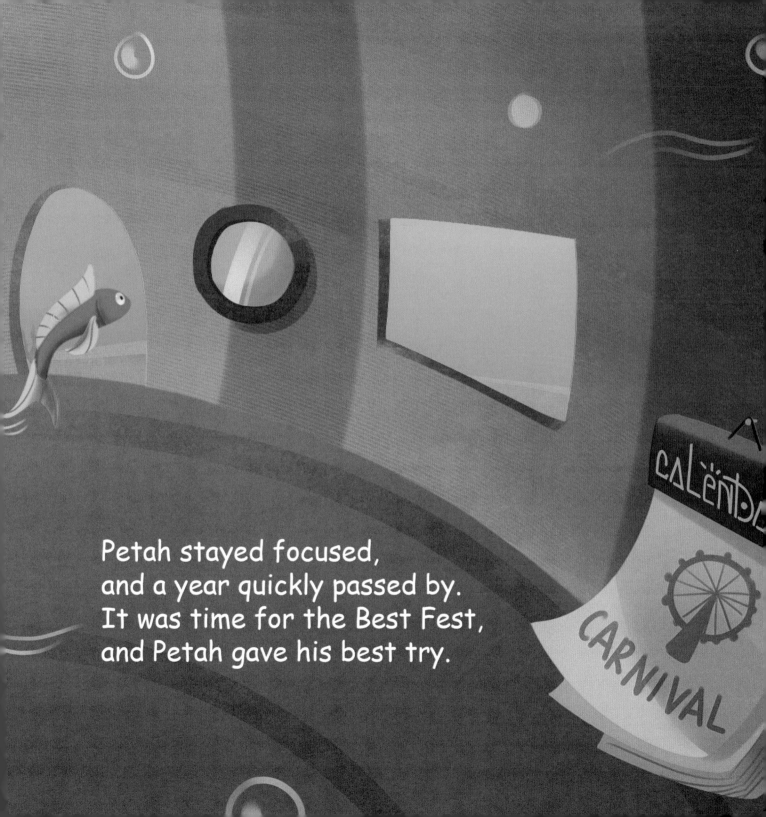

Petah stayed focused,
and a year quickly passed by.
It was time for the Best Fest,
and Petah gave his best try.

When Petah arrived,
he saw Reynard and the twins.
Petah was now the best scrubber ever.
His friends hoped he would win.

Queen Fish read from the scroll.
"Oh, what could be sweeta'?
The first ticket to the Big Blue Sea
goes to..."

The End

Look for more exciting adventures from the Big Blue Sea...

Sheena
and the
Big Blue Sea

and...

Reynard Works Hard
a Big Blue Sea book

Made in the USA
Middletown, DE
12 June 2021